Broom Mates

By Margie Palatini ☆ Illustrated by Howard Fine

Hyperion Books for Children
New York

Library of Congress Cataloging-in-Publication Data
Palatini, Margie.
Broom mates / by Margie Palatini; illustrated by Howard Fine.—1st ed.
p.   cm.
Summary: Gritch the Witch is not pleased when her sister, Mag the Hag,
shows up early for the Halloween party.
ISBN 0-7868-0418-1
[1. Witches—Fiction. 2. Sisters—Fiction. 3. Humorous stories.] I. Fine, Howard, ill. II. Title.
PZ7.P1755 Br 2003
[E]—dc21
2001016956

Visit www.hyperionchildrensbooks.com

With love and ha-has, for my sister, best friend, and former broom mate
—M.P.

For Emma, the newest broom mate
—H.F.

ritch the Witch was grouchy, grumpy, and pooped. Getting ready for her big howliday party had just plain tuckered her out.

"Yikes!" she shrieked, eyeing herself in her witch-watching mirror. "I'd better get some beauty sleep."

"Try twenty years," the mirror cracked.

You're Invited

With a yawn and a yank, Gritch pulled on her jammies, shooed out the bedbugs, and headed for beddy-bye.

She was already sawing z's and counting lamb chops, when—wouldn't you know it—

Eeeee-aaaAAAHHhhh!

the doorbell screamed.

What a nightmare.

"Get your thumping thumb off that buzzard's button, you bell-ringing busybody!" grumbled Gritch. "Scoot! Scram! Skedaddle!"

"Skedaddle nothing, sister!" came the call from the other side of the knocker. "Yoo-hoo! Guess who? Just flew in from Maliboo."

The door flew open with a windy whoosh. The bell-ringing busybody was none other than her saucy, bossy sister, Mag the Hag. "You're a fright for sore eyes!" snorted Gritch.

"You can still scare the hair off a hare yourself, sissy," cackled her sister. "I have a little Mag lag, but I'm ready to party hearty."

Egads. Gritch groaned. "The party, smarty—isn't until—*tomorrow*!"

"No *problemo*!" Mag sang out. "I'll just bunk here tonight with you, *broom mate*!"

Drat. Gritch gritted her tooth. Having the hag come home for the howlidays was not going to be a treat. The sisters just did not get along, no how, no way, not ever. They had fussed and feuded about anything and everything ever since they were little ghouls. Broomin' with Mag was not going to be easy, even if it was just for one day.

Gritch grumbled. "That hag is always in my face, not to mention my space."

"Point these beauteous blinkers to a pillow, broomie," Mag called from the hall. "*Moi* needs some shut-eye."

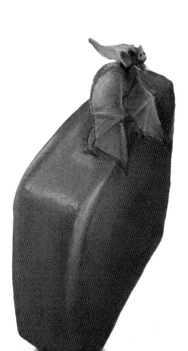

The hag dropped with a plop, snuggled, and sighed.
"Not too big. Not too little. *Just right.*"
"WRONG!" groused Gritch. "Look who's sleeping in *my* bed!
And I'm not talking Goldilocks!"

"Well, here I am now," snorted Mag, lathering her face with fright cream.

"Just stay on your own side, you bed-hoggin' hag," Gritch groused and crawled into bed.

"Gladly, you ol' sleepin' bag," muttered Mag with a yank. "But now *you* have all the covers."

Gritch whined, "And like always, you took all the lumps!"

"*O-o-oh*, you want lumps, do you?" Mag grabbed her pillow. "I don't remember. . . . Do you like one lump or two?"

Ding! Ding! Ding!

The girls came out swinging.

Feathers started to fly.

They finally knocked each other out during round three.

"I'm telling Mummy on you," snored Mag, spitting feathers.

"I'm telling on you," snoozed Gritch with a head full of lumps.

The next morning, the broom mates *both* got up on the wrong side of the bed. They were already squabbling and squawking before their first sip of hot flea.

Decorating for the party was a disaster.

Gritch wanted the spiders dangling. Mag wanted the webs tangling.

Everything got tied up in knots.

Mag wanted the pumpkins squished. Gritch wanted the pumpkins squashed.

SQUISH! SQUASH! SPLAT!

And then there was a dust brawl.

"Clearly, drearie, you are a flop with the mop," declared Mag.

"You're the bust when it comes to dust, sister," coughed Gritch.

Things *really* got down and dirty.

Dust bunnies were hopping all over the place.

Mag brushed herself off with a haughty *harumph*.

"I'm going to do some spelling," she said with a wave of a wand. "Mummy always said *I* was the best speller in the family."

"You? Get a grip," muttered Gritch. "*I* can spell anything better than you!"

Poof. "No you can't!"

Poof. "Yes I can!"

Poof. "No you can't!"

Poof. POOF. CRASH!

"Uh-ohhh," said Gritch, stepping over broken spells. "Mummy's going to be mad at *yoo-oo.*"

Mag sputtered and stomped off to the kitchen. "Phooey! I'm going to make my rat-tail-tooey."

Gritch hurried to tie on her apron first. It was almost the witching hour, and her guests would be arriving any moment. "Your tooey is a bunch of hooey. My brew-ha-ha will be the howl of the party."

The girls glared at each other. Squinted. Grinned. Cackled.

"Cooking contest!"

A squirm of worm. A slush of mush. A bit of spit. *Voilà!*

"Dee-lish!" said Mag, stirring her stew.

"Yes, your rat-tail-tooey is terribly . . . tasty," said Gritch, lapping up a spoonful. "But Mummy always said my brew-ha-ha was absolute *perfection*!"

Mag held her nose. She slurped. She shrugged.

"Eh . . . Could use a hint of hee-hee."

Gritch almost choked on her ha-ha. "My ha-ha needs hee-hee? Ha!"

"Hee-hee," repeated Mag with a burp. "You could throw in some ho-ho, too."

"Ho-ho, too?" said Gritch. "How about if I throw in *you*?"

SPLASH!

"Ooo-Ooow!" yowled Mag.

Gritch doubled over in a cackle. Yes, ma'am.
Just what her brew-ha-ha needed—
one big, old howl!

Mag came up for air. "Hardy-har-har!"

"Ho, ho, ho," Gritch chuckled. Then she
slipped. And slid. "Oh, no, no, NO!"

Kerplunk!

Knock! Knock!

The broom mates bobbed up from the brew. Blubbered. Gasped.
"MUMMY!"
Their mummy was not at all pleased and looked *very* unraveled.
Gritch shivered and shook. Mag quivered and quaked.
Mummy was silent. Very, very silent.

Then she gave the surprised, soggy sisters a hug and called out, "Trick or treat!"

Gritch looked at Mag and giggled. "Trick?"

Mag looked at Gritch and chuckled. "Treat?"

Mummy laughed. "That's what I like to *see*. Sharing, scaring, and no problems."

The sisters promised to be on their best beastly behavior.

"Naughty, but nice," ordered Mummy. "Now, let's party."

"Remember, Mummy knows best!"